1

ELEPHANTS IN THE LIVING ROOM

Written by Shannon Fay
with
Illustrations by Danny Deeptown

This production 2016
ISBN: 1522754806
ISBN-13:978-1522754800

Text © Shannon Fay 2015
Illustrations © Danny Deeptown 2015

To my amazing family,
for always listening to my stories,
and especially Mama, my first and biggest fan of all.
Shannon

To my mum,
for teaching me to hold a pencil your way,
the best way.
Danny

1. What is that smell?

Nothing in Cody's life made sense right now. The cookies were stale and the milk was like chalky water. He couldn't find anything he wanted in his house. His parents were acting all weird, and his sister was weirder than ever. And now, on top of everything else, something in the house smelled really, really bad. Funky.

Can't a guy just sit and eat his cookies?' he wondered. 'Is that too much to ask?' The smell was ruining his already-not-so-great after-school snack. Why did everything always happen at the same time, and what was that funky smell?

It smelled kind of familiar. Still munching a cookie, Cody followed his nose to the living room. What he saw there stopped him dead in his tracks. His cookie fell to the floor, and he yelled at the top of his lungs. "Mom! Mommmmmmmmm!!!"

"What's all the commotion, Cody? I'm upstairs, packing," his mother called out. "You know you aren't supposed to yell in the house, young man. You just come up here, if you want to talk to me."

Cody turned and bounded up the stairs as fast as he could, skipping every other step. Boom, boom, boom, boom, boom. "Mom," he gasped, "in – the – living – room – you - gotta –

come - see. C'mon," he tugged on her arm, "PLEASE. You gotta come see this!"

"Oh, for heaven's sake, Cody." His mom sounded aggravated. "You sound like an *elephant* coming up those stairs. Can't you see I'm right in the middle of packing? I'll be down in a few minutes."

Cody grabbed her arm again, pleading. "Mom, I mean it. *Seriously.* You gotta come see this! RIGHT NOW!"

She put down the roll of tape impatiently. "Well, what on earth is it?"

"It IS an elephant!" Cody waved his arms in the air. "IN! OUR! LIVING ROOM!"

2. The elephant by the coffee table

Cody took off, running back down the stairs to the living room. Sure enough, there it was, still standing there, big as a . . . well, big as an elephant! It was right there, just standing there next to the coffee table. Cody shook his head in disbelief. The elephant looked around at him and winked.

Cody started to yelp again, but he felt his mother's eyes on him. He turned around and saw her staring at him, her jaw clinched and her arms folded. Not a good sign.

"Cody Jason Glockenspiel. I am not happy with you, young man."

Oh, right, like he couldn't tell that. "But Mom," Cody asked, "don't you see it?"He was so confused.

"What I see is a very silly boy who doesn't

seem to care how much trouble he causes anyone else. Couldn't you see how busy I was? Couldn't you see I didn't have time for any of your little games?"

"But . . . the elephant . . . can't you see it?"

"Cody, didn't I just tell you that I don't have time for any more games? Please, Honey. Let me get finished packing up the guest bedroom, and then you can talk to me while I get dinner ready."

His mother turned impatiently and left the room. Cody just stood there for a moment, frozen. 'What is this, some kind of joke?' he thought. 'A bad dream?' He pinched himself. "Ouch!" Nope, he was awake, alright.

It sure looked like a real elephant. Cody couldn't just stand there blinking all day. He had to figure this out. He put one hand over his eyes and stretched the other out in front of him, then took a deep breath and began to inch forward. He took little baby steps, like he was afraid to hit his shins. But that wasn't what he was afraid of.

He inched closer and closer to the coffee table, scooching his feet on the carpet. Finally, his fingers were barely touching something.

He stopped for just a second, took another deep breath and then forced himself to reach even further.

No sir, this was no joke. It was not a bad dream. It was 100% real. Right there in his own hand was the bristly, wrinkly hide of an elephant!

Cody peeked between his fingers, and then dropped his hand. It wasn't really all that scary, now that he was touching it. Actually, it was kind of cool being that close to a real elephant, and anyway, the elephant seemed nice enough and all.

What was scary was that it was right HERE - - right here in his very own living room. And what was even scarier than that, was that his mother acted like she couldn't SEE it.

How could anyone NOT see an elephant in the living room?

Cody backed away from the elephant slowly, still waiting for it to disappear, or do something. But it just stood there quietly, one big, wrinkly eye watching Cody watch it.

As he turned the corner into the kitchen, it winked at him again.

3. Don't bother your father

He got some more milk and another Oreo. He knew he wasn't supposed to have more than three, but a guy can't think on an empty stomach, right? It was kind of funny, but just a few minutes ago, he thought the worst problem in his life was that his family was moving. Or, maybe, that the cookies were stale.

Trying to figure out exactly when everything had gone crazy, Cody thought back to the ride home. Nothing strange there, except that he almost missed his stop because he was thinking about stuff. Or, maybe he was trying not to think.

He'd gotten off of the bus and waved good-bye to Mr. Thompson, just like he did every day. Then he'd walked up the path to his house, just like he had for four years, ever since he started kindergarten.

He'd stood there for a few minutes, staring at the "For Sale" sign in the yard. He hated it. It was planted right in the middle of the yard, messing up any chance for a game of soccer. And it was crooked. He'd kicked it as hard as he could and gone in the front door, watching it swing wildly on its hooks.

Ka-thunk! He'd fallen over a cardboard box. His books scattered across the floor. It seemed like there were more boxes every day. He didn't know they even had this much stuff. Plus, he didn't know why they had to move.

Nobody else even seemed to care but him. His sister thought it was ex-cit-ing. 'What does she know?' Cody thought. 'She doesn't have any friends, anyway.' His mother was too busy looking for another house and making lists to even think about it. Even his dad was too busy finishing up

the big project at work, the one that got him the dumb promotion, the one that was causing them to move all the way to the other side of town in the first place.

His mother said he shouldn't complain about moving, or it would make his dad feel bad. More than anything, Cody wouldn't want to make his dad feel bad. But what's a guy supposed to do? See, his dad was the one that Cody always talked to when he was upset, and now he couldn't talk to his dad because it was *about* his dad.

'Why can't everything stay the same?' he thought. 'Why can't Dad just stay at this office in this side of town so I can stay in my own school, in my own bedroom, in my own soccer league?'

Why did all of these problems have to happen at one time? And then there was the biggest problem of all, of course- -the elephant in the living room!

4. And the one with the tutu

Cody got two more cookies. This was an emergency, after all. They didn't help, though- -his brain was blank. So he had one more and made a list of possibilities:

THE ELEPHANT LIST

1. The elephant escaped from the zoo. (But then, he scratched that out. It would have been on the news, for sure.)

2. The elephant escaped from the circus. (But then,he scratched that out, because there was no circus in town right now.)

3. The elephant isn't really there (But then he scratched that out, too - just because...)

'Because that means I'm crazy, right?'

He stood up quietly and snuck over to the doorway, then peeked in to check. The elephant

wasn't over by the coffee table anymore! A big
smile spread across his face . . . until he realized that
it wasn't gone. It was standing right on the other side
of the doorway! The elephant winked and grabbed
the last cookie out of his hand, then lumbered back
to the coffee table, munching.

Cody sighed, went back to the kitchen and
washed the slimy elephant stuff off of his hand.
'Yuk!' he thought, as he sat down to try to do his
homework. Even homework was better than thinking
about the elephant in the living room.

He couldn't really concentrate, though, and he
hadn't gotten much done when he heard his sister,
Camilla,coming in from school. "Hi, Mom!" she
yelled up the stairs.

"Hi, Sweetie!" his mom called back.

What did she see in Little Miss Perfect, anyway? 'It's more like, 'Little Miss Perfectly Fake.'
He was still laughing at his own joke when she came

into the kitchen.

"You are soooo gross, Cody," she greeted him. "What did you do in here, anyway? It smells like a zoo."

"Hey! Come with me!" Cody jumped up, desperate for someone to help explain the situation.

"No way. I'm gonna tell Mom you're using your chemistry set inside again."

"Really! You gotta see this!" He grabbed her by the book bag and pulled her into the living room.

"Hey, cut it out!" Camilla squealed.

Cody stood in the living room with his hands on his hips, like he'd just won a prize. "There, see? What'd I tell you?"

But Camilla just looked blankly at the room and said, "What?"

Poor Cody felt like a balloon with a hole in it. Shhh-hhhh-hhhhh. "Don't you see it?"

"See what? You are so weird. So the living room's still not packed. Mom said she's going to pack it up last, Uber-goober." He hated it when she called him that, but right now, he would kiss her if she'd just help him out.

"Camilla. Really. Don't you see the elephant?" he pleaded. "Pleeeease tell me you see it."

"Yeah, right, Cody. Sure, I see an elephant. It's dancing over by the fireplace, with the lampshade on its head." She shrugged his hand off of her book bag and turned to walk out. "Boy, are you nuts."

Cody watched her walk out of the room and then turned around to face the elephant again.

It was still there, alright, just standing there by the coffee table, watching him. But now, as if that wasn't bad enough - - there was another one! This one had on a pink tutu, and was dancing by the fire-place, wearing the lampshade on its head!

"Aaaaaaah!!" He ran screaming from the room.

5. Double Trouble

Cody couldn't seem to catch his breath, so he headed outside to get some fresh air. He was almost to the front door when it opened, and his dad stepped in. For a moment, he felt better. Now that his dad was home, maybe everything was going to be okay.

"Well, hi there, Son," his dad said, as he hung up his coat. "What's the word?" His dad asked him that every day when he got home. Cody knew it meant, 'what's going on?', but he usually made up a word, like, 'glockenable' or 'fantastaspiel' to make his dad laugh.

Today, though, Cody could only stand there. He wasn't able to make himself say the word, "Elephanterrible."

"Hey, how about a little soccer after I

read the paper?" Cody just stood there like a zombie, but his dad didn't get it.

"Oh, I guess you're right," said his dad, "I forgot about the "For Sale" sign. Well, maybe I can get the real estate agent to move it over a little tomorrow." His dad patted him on the back absently as he unfolded the paper and walked into the living room. Cody stood in the hallway waiting for his father to scream or faint or something.

But there was nothing; his father didn't make a single sound except for the rustling of the newspaper.

Cody sat down on the stairs for a minute. He fought back tears for the first time in years - - like, since he was five years old and broke his arm on the jungle gym. He sat there for what seemed like hours, until his bottom went numb, trying hard to think, trying even harder not to cry.

Finally, he got up and plodded into the

living room.

There was the elephant, alright, still standing next to the coffee table. There was the other elephant, too, still dancing by the fireplace, wearing the lampshade for a hat. And there was his dad, just sitting there in his favorite chair, reading the newspaper under a lamp with no lampshade, as if nothing strange was happening at all.

Cody sat down with a heavy thunk on the edge of the coffee table and stared at his dad, silently begging him to say something, *anything* about the elephants. His heart jumped when his father looked up over the newspaper. Cody crossed his fingers.

"Son. . ."

"Yes, Sir?" Cody asked, hopefully.

"Do you know what happened to the lampshade?"

His heart sank again as he looked over at the

elephant wearing it. He shook his head. 'Okay, that proves it-- no one else can see the elephants,' he thought. 'No one.'

He'd hoped that his mother was just too busy and that his sister was just teasing him. But, no.

It didn't matter if there was nothing on the news about a zoo escape. It didn't matter if there was no circus in town. It didn't matter that Cody couldn't find a good reason why the elephants were here, because, if no one else could see them, it meant that it must be #3 on The Elephant List- -he must be crazy.

"No, Sir," he told his dad sadly. "I guess I don't really know what happened to the lampshade."

At least he was honest -- he really wasn't too sure about anything, anymore. Cody struggled to his feet, his mind spinning. On his way out of the

living room, he noticed a huge lump behind the curtains.
He closed his eyes, held his breath, and pulled the
curtains aside.

'I must be getting crazier by the minute,' he
thought, looking sadly at yet another elephant. The
new elephant blew a big, wet raspberry at him.
Thpbthpbth! Cody wiped his face and let the
curtain drop back into place. He tripped over a
lump in the carpet, and discovered the twin of the
raspberry blower. He greeted Cody the same way,
Thpbthpbthpbth!

Poor Cody slowly wiped his face again and
hobbled back to the kitchen. 'We're infested!'

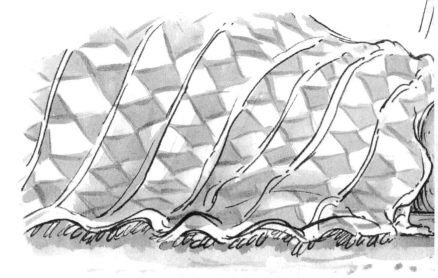

6. Cody the Comedian

Cody gathered up his books, and went upstairs to try to concentrate on his homework. Elephants or no elephants, crazy or not, he had a multiplication test the next day, and he didn't really know his nine-times very well. Plus, there was a book report due.

He went through his flash cards and wrote the nine-times nine times, and then practiced the old finger trick just for good measure, but he always ran out of fingers before he got to 9 X 12.

He started his book report, but every other word he wrote was "crazy," or "elephant." It was no use, his brain was mush. He gave up and lay back on the floor. He could smell something coming from the kitchen, but it was something good this time, so he went downstairs. "Perfect timing, dinner's on the table," his mom said, and she ruffled his hair, which, by the way, he totally hated. "Sorry about this afternoon. I was just really busy and got annoyed by your little joke."

"But, Mom," he said, "I wasn't joking," This was getting seriously depressing.

"Oh, Cody. You are funny - - what a little comedian." And she ruffled his hair again.

At the table, his sister was talking about her day at school. She'd gotten another A+ on a math test, of course, and was up for lead of the play. Cody made a rude noise with his mouth, but his sister ignored him. "I told them that I couldn't really promise I'd take the lead, since we'll be moving and all," she said primly, wiping her mouth, "but then Mrs. Carter said they'll even move the date of the play, if they have to. Just so I can play Eliza!"

'Gag me.' Cody thought, as he took a bite

of his meatloaf, but he could hardly swallow it.

'For real- -gag me!' It tasted super dry, almost crunchy, like Styrofoam with ketchup on it. And there was still the smell of a three-week - old circus tent in the air. It was too disgusting. He put his fork down and watched the others eat like nothing was wrong.

"Mmm, mmm. Great meatloaf, Honey," said his dad. Cody just shook his head. The meatloaf was terrible. What was up with these people?

"Hey, Dad. You won't believe what Cody said today," Camilla began.

"Oh, no. Did he play his little joke on you, too?" asked his mother.

Camilla pointed with her fork at Cody and laughed, "He thinks there's an elephant in the living room!"

His father grinned and said, "Well, I didn't see any elephant, but does anyone know what happened to the lampshade?"

His mother looked accusingly at Cody. "Cody,?"

"Ma'am?" he asked, miserably.

"Do you know what happened to the lampshade?"

His father shook his head. "I already asked. He said he doesn't know."

His mother narrowed her eyes. "Cody? Is that the whole truth?"

Cody hung his head. "Well, um, actually, the last time I saw it," he swallowed hard, "one of the elephants was wearing it." His family exploded with laughter. Cody shook his head slowly. Nobody got it. "It was wearing a tutu and dancing by the fireplace."

His mother and father almost choked with laughter, but his sister poked him and said, "Hey, that was my line!"

Cody and Camilla cleared the table while

his parents put the left-overs away. 'Great,' Cody thought, 'crunchy meatloaf sandwiches tomorrow. Yum, yum, yuk.'

They finished the dishes and went to watch their favorite Tuesday night show. But when they walked into the living room, Cody knew there was no way.

The elephant by the fireplace was still doing pirouettes and other ballerina stuff. The elephant behind the curtain was playing hide and seek with its twin. Not to mention the fact that there still happened to be a big, fat one, right in the middle of the room, next to the coffee table, blocking the TV!

"Where are you going, Son?" his father asked. "It's your favorite show."

"I've got to finish my book report, Dad. And, anyway, I can't see the TV because of the elephant." He left the room to the sound of their laughter, as they turned up the television.

7. Wake me up, please!

When Cody opened his eyes the next morning, he hoped it was all just a bad dream. But as he came around the corner of the living room, his hopes were ruined. They were all still there, in their cute little jammies, snug as a bunch of bugs-in -a-rug, cuddled under the carpet. 'Someone, *anyone*, PLEASE wake me up!' he thought. This was the longest, worst nightmare he'd ever had.

He dropped his book bag and stood there watching, still amazed. The sleepy elephants began to stretch and yawn, rubbing their eyes. There was another new one today- - with cool designer sunglasses- -and he looked over the top of them at Cody and waved at him with his big ears. 'Well, at least they're friendly,' he thought.

He went to sit at the kitchen table, the smell

almost choking him, and pretended not to listen to the noise coming from the other room. It sounded like elephants playing soccer, and it probably was. Rumble, fumble, tumble, Goal! His mother turned from the coffee pot, seemingly deaf to the racket. "Cody, I might be gone when you get home today. I think I found our new house."

'That's good,' thought Cody, 'because with all those elephants, we're sure going to need a new house.'

"I'll leave the key under the mat and be home by dinner. And, Mrs. Jones is just next door. Maybe we'll do pizza- - would you like that?"

'Better than crunchy meatloaf,' he thought. 'Ha! Dodged that bullet!'

"Oh, and I made you a sandwich from the left-over meatloaf for your lunch."

'Well, almost.' He smiled politely. "Thanks, Mom."

"You're welcome," she beamed. "I know it's your favorite. Okay, now, make sure you do your homework before you turn on the TV, okay? Your sister has play audition, so she won't be home, either. And, not too many Oreos. Don't think I didn't notice that you didn't eat your dinner last night and the cookie jar is half empty."

Cody just sat there, staring straight ahead.

"Hey," she said, "are you okay? You seem quiet. Is something bothering you?"

'Just the elephants in the living room,' he thought, but all he said was, "Big math test today."

"Oh, Honey, don't worry so much. You've been studying- - I'm sure you'll do just fine."

She ruffled his hair and walked out of the room, "I know I can trust you, Cody. Good luck on your test."

Cody tried to unruffle his hair and headed back into the living room to get his book bag.

Just as he got to the doorway, the bag whizzed through the air past his face and was caught by one of the twins. Fmmmp! He chased the twins, but they tossed it over his head to the new one with the sunglasses.

Cody caught a strap and pulled, but the elephant pulled even harder, and then the zipper broke and all of his homework tumbled out. The one in the tutu grabbed some of the papers and started making confetti- - out of his book report! He got as many pieces as he could and headed out of the door to catch his bus.

'Man.' He shook his head. 'Sometimes it just doesn't pay to get out of bed.'

8. The Truth Hurts

Cody couldn't keep his mind on anything at school, no big surprise. He failed the nine-times, even though he knew them backwards and forwards by now. Well, he would have done okay if the teacher would've let him use his fingers. 'What a gyp, he thought. 'The only times-table with a trick, and she wouldn't even let me use it.'

He was so anxious, he didn't even have the heart to play soccer at recess, and when Tim kicked the ball at him, it hit him right in the head.

"Man, you really blew that one! You could've scored a goal for sure!" said Tim, as the bell rang. "What's up with you today?"

Cody looked at his best friend in the whole wide world. He really needed someone to believe him. He took a deep breath. "What would you say if I told you that there were five elephants in my living room?" he asked.

Tim punched him in the shoulder and laughed like a donkey. "Eeey-yaww!" He punched him again. "Man, I am sooooo gonna miss you! You are the funniest guy I know! Eeey-yaw! Elephants! Where do you come up with this stuff?"

But Cody didn't exactly feel funny. Not "haha" funny, anyway. Miss Stuart told them to take their seats. She narrowed her eyes and raised that one evil eyebrow and gave Tim the famous "Look." He knew what that meant, and scrambled into his desk, eyes straight ahead. She asked them to pass their book reports up to the front.

Cody raised his hand. "Miss Stuart? Could I borrow some tape?" He had arranged all of the pieces of his book report on his desk.

"Cody! What on earth happened to your book report?" He looked down at his desk miserably.

The trouble with folks asking questions like that was, if he told the truth, they were going to laugh or call him a liar, or maybe even give him an F minus on a book report. But Cody really, really liked telling the truth. It was a lot easier than trying to remember exactly what the fib was, and who he'd told it to.

"Cody?"

He took another deep breath and stared at his feet. "One of the elephants tore it up."

"Did you say, 'an elephant?'" Miss Stuart raised her left eyebrow. "What elephant?"
This wasn't getting any better. "The one with the tutu."

Tim started laughing and then the whole class was cracking up and Miss Stuart gave them all the "Look." She plopped the tape dispenser down on his desk with a thud and announced that everyone could plan to stay inside for second recess.

A loud, "Aaaa-aaaw-wwww. . .," went up, but she just shrugged and said, "Well, I guess you can thank Cody - - or maybe his elephant."

9. Gimme a break!

There was no one around when Cody got home, and he remembered his mother was looking at new houses. But, he knew right away that something bad had happened. The smell was worse, the noise was worse, and he just knew . . . .

The living room was a mess. The twins had taken down the curtains to wear as capes, and they were jumping off of the coffee table, trying to fly. The elephant by the coffee table, and the cool one with the sunglasses had joined trunks so the one in the tutu could use them to jump rope. Ka-boom, ka-boom, ka-boom! Every time she jumped, the whole room bounced. Cody just barely caught the lamp as it fell off of the table.

There was a loud crrrrrraaaack as the twins launched themselves from the coffee table and it broke right down the middle.

Cody stood there, frozen, for a moment, amazed, amused, and yet terrified, too. He really didn't know what to do. "Hey!" he yelled. "Cut it out!" The elephants all paused for just a moment before falling to the floor, laughing and rolling around. 'Well, that sure worked. Not.' Maybe he should get Miss Stuart to come give them the "Look."

He dragged his book bag to the kitchen and got some Oreos, but he couldn't eat even a single one. 'Gimme a break!' he thought. What was he supposed to do, anyway? He was just a kid and no one would listen to him. 'Everyone thinks I'm crazy and now I'm going to get in trouble because the dumb elephants broke everything.'

He almost smiled at his own joke. 'That's not the kind of break I meant.' He walked back to the living room, Oreo in hand, and the elephant by

coffee table lumbered over to try to grab it.

Suddenly, Cody's eyes got wide. He had an idea! He held the cookie up for the elephant to see, and then started backing away. Slowly, slowly, he backed up through the living room door to the kitchen, then through the back door into the yard. It worked! The elephant followed him outside!

10. Cody to the Rescue

Cody gave the elephant the cookie, then ran inside to get some more. He gave the elephant the whole bag to keep him busy, and while he pigged out, Cody tied his leg to his mother's lilac bush. One down, four more to go . . . . He felt like a superhero! 'Woohoo!'

Cody ran back inside, to see what he could find to lure the others outside. He tried peanuts, corn chips, apples, even gummy worms, but none of the other elephants would follow him.

The twins were still wearing their capes, but now they were throwing the sofa pillow at each other. Cody snapped his fingers and ran to his room to get his new ball. When they saw it, their eyes sparkled, and they followed him into the front yard. Cody didn't think it mattered about the neighbors, since no one else seemed to be able to see them anyway. He got them started playing and then snuck away to see about the others.

Hmmm. What could he do about the one in the tutu? He went into his sister's room and found the perfect thing - - one of those little Miss America crown thingies, a tiara. When she saw it, she nearly dropped the mirror she was holding. She followed him, turning little pirouettes, into the garage. Cody put the tiara in the middle of the floor and when she went for it, he left and locked the garage door. It was working! He only had one more to go and he'd be rid of the elephants!

Back in the house, he sat and watched the one with the sunglasses. The elephant was just sitting in his father's chair, chilling, tapping out a little rhythm on the arm of the chair with his trunk. Ta-dum, ta-dum, ta-da-dum. Very cool- -a musical elephant. That gave Cody an idea and he ran up to get his MP3 player. It was a birthday present, and he hated the thought of anything happening to it, but this was an emergency.

It worked like a charm, once he finally got the little ear buds to stay in the elephant's big ears.

Cody left him on the back porch, swaying to the music, flapping his ears and tapping his trunk on the banister. Cody snuck back inside and locked all of the doors and windows.

He did his best to straighten up the living room, and then strutted back into the kitchen, with a swipe of his hands. Success!

He really wanted an Oreo now, but they were all gone, so he settled on milk and corn chips - - not the same thing, by the way, but he figured it was a small price to pay.

Cody had just pulled out his homework, when he heard a sickening noise in the living room. Rumble, fumble, tumble, craaaaack, ta-dum, ta-da-dum, da-dum-dum. It couldn't be, right? NO! He ran to the doorway of the living room, baffled.

Every one of them was back. How had they . . .when. . . why? WHY??

To make matters worse, if matters could be worse, the one from the backyard still had his leg tied to the lilac bush, only now the whole bush was in the living room, dirt and roots and all. And the twins were still throwing the soccerball- - IN THE LIVING ROOM!

Cody couldn't stand it anymore. It was too much. He dragged himself up to his room and lay down on his bed to wait for someone else to come home and help. He didn't care who- - someone, anyone, even his sister. All he knew was that he couldn't fix this on his own.

11. Crazy Cody

It just so happened that his whole family arrived at the same time - - too late, of course. His mother had picked Camilla up, and they walked in just as Dad got home. Cody waited, listening at his door. Murmurs from the living room drew him downstairs, and he stopped in the hallway.

"What in heaven's name do you think he's done here?" asked his mother. "Has he lost his mind?"

"This is pretty serious, Hon," answered his dad, "Maybe we should consider calling a psychiatrist or something."

Camilla came around the corner and grinned evilly at him. "Mom and Dad want you, right NOW. Boy, are you ever in trouble!"

And she skipped up the stairs, cheerfully.

"I told you- - you're nuts!"

Cody could barely bring himself to go into the living room. His parents were sitting together on the sofa looking grim.

His dad's chair was once again occupied by the elephant with the sunglasses on. He seemed to be napping, his trunk draped over the arm of the chair. 'Awwww, did the iddy widdle ewephant have a wough day?' thought Cody, sarcastically. 'Poor baby. . . .'

The twins were playing marbles in the corner, and the one with the tutu was drawing a picture on the wall with a purple crayon she held in her trunk.

"Sit down, Son. We need to talk to you," his dad said sternly. Cody looked for a place to sit, but since there wasn't anywhere left, he finally settled on the floor.

"I just don't understand, Cody." His mother .

sniffed sadly. "I asked you to take care of things today while I was gone. I trusted you, and now just look at this . . . this mess," she said, tears in her eyes. "How are we ever going to sell the house like this?"

His dad put his arms around her. "Alright, Son," his dad began, "I'm going to ask you one time, and one time only--what happened in here today? And I expect you to tell me the truth."

Cody stared at his parents, then at the elephants, and then at his parents again. He was so confused. If they couldn't see the elephants, then how were they going to believe the truth? His dad was staring back, waiting. "Son?"

This wasn't going to go well, he just knew it. He gulped. "The, uh, the elephants did it."

His parents just stared at him for a moment, then his dad said, "Alright, go to your room. Just go. I can't tell you how disappointed I am in you,

Cody. The rest of us are going to dinner to celebrate your sister's lead in the play and the fact that Mom found a new house for us.

We'll bring you home some left - over pizza. Maybe."

12. Curtains for Cody

While his family was gone, Cody stayed in his room. He could hear music from the living room, and he was pretty sure it was the Chicken Dance. That was a pretty funny thought, elephants doing the Chicken Dance, and he really wanted to go down to watch them, but he stayed in his room.

All of his life, his dad had listened to him. He had always felt as though he could tell him anything, anything at all. Until now. He buried his head in his pillow and finally let the tears go.

Here he was, with the biggest problem of his life, and there was no one to help him.

The elephants had ruined his house and his parents trust in him. He'd be lucky if they didn't put him in a loony bin for being crazy.

He was scared. He was all alone. And had

run out of ideas.

After about a million years, his family came home and called him down. His dad was sitting on what was left of his chair. His mother had a cup of tea perched on the arm of the sofa, and her eyes were still red. The one by the coffee table was eating his left over pizza.

His sister was sitting on the trunk of the elephant by the coffee table, swinging her legs and watching TV, eating ice cream. No one was talking.

The elephant in the tutu was doing pirouettes again, and one of the twins was pulling the lamp switch: on, off, on, off. . . . The other twin was hiding behind the curtain, and suddenly, the room was filled with the most awful smell ever!

Cody had been to the circus; he'd seen the pooper scoopers, and he knew what that smell was!

"That's IT!" he yelled at the top of his lungs. "You are ruining EVERYTHING!"

13. Cody Comes Clean

His dad glanced up from his paper. "What do you mean, Son? Is this about the move? Is that what all of this is about?" His mother gave him that look, that what-did-I-tell-you look.

"Cody, don't you want to move?" his dad asked, drawing him nearer.

He avoided his mother's eyes as he answered, "Well... no, Sir. I don't."

"Why didn't you talk to me about this? Haven't I always listened? Haven't I always told you that you could come to me with anything?"

"Yes, Sir. But I didn't want, you know, to hurt your feelings or anything." His father shook his head.

"Cody, I don't have to move to take that job. I just thought it might be a nice change for us, since it pays better. Make new friends, get a bigger house, you know." He looked at his wife. "Hon?" "Do you want to move?"

"Well," she shrugged, "I have to admit, I've always loved this house. I had my babies here, and I like the schools and my bridge group - -oh, and there's my yoga class and . . . ."

He hugged her. "Okay, okay. I get it."

"Camilla? What's your vote?"

"Can I still have new bedroom furniture?" She didn't even turn around.

Dad rolled his eyes, not bothering to respond. He hugged his son tightly and said, "There, that wasn't so bad, was it? But, I will tell you what really hurts my feelings - - that you didn't come to me with this. Promise me that won't ever happen again, okay?"

Cody looked around the room. The twins were about to do a double tumbleset into the TV.

"You want me to tell you when I'm upset?"
His dad hugged him tighter. "Absolutely."
"Even if it isn't something you want to hear?"
"*Especially* if it's something I don't want
to hear."

14. Truth or Dare

Cody took a deep breath. Whenever he played Truth or Dare with Tim, he always took the dare - - it was a lot more fun. But this time, the truth *was* the dare. He didn't think it was going to be much fun, one way or the other.

"Dad," he said, "there are five elephants in this room, and they're making a mess."

All of the elephants stopped dead in their tracks, and stared at Cody. They stared at Dad. Dad blinked his eyes and looked around.

"Well, that certainly explains the terrible smell in here."

The twins looked up, annoyed. They really wanted to do that tumbleset. But, instead, they shrugged, linked arms and legs, and did the monster-walk over to the window. Ba-boom,

ba-boom, ba-boom! One twin boosted the other
one up and then scrambled out of the window, too.
They stuck their trunks in for one last "Thpbthpbth!"
and then they were gone.

Cody looked over at his mother. The
elephant in the tutu was drinking her tea, slurping it
up through her trunk. *Schllllluuup*. The elephant
burped. His mother stared at the empty cup for a
minute, then said, "Oh, my." She looked around
the room, dazed, and then frowned. "Oh, my..."
she repeated, then put her hands on her hips and
said, "Okay guys, the party's over. You . . . you
elephants have got to go."

The one in the sunglasses raised his shades,
looked at Cody, and winked. He sauntered out of
the door, holding it open for the one in the tutu,
who blew a kiss to them all as she danced out on
her toes.

Camilla still sat on the trunk of the one by

the coffee table, swinging her legs and eating her ice cream. She glanced around, wide-eyed. "Elephants? I don't see any elephants. I don't know *what* you mean."

"Camilla Prudence Glockenspiel." His mother was standing with her arms crossed. "Get off of that elephant. This minute."

But before Camilla could get down, the elephant dumped her right on the floor, Thunk! and lumbered toward the door. Camilla was sprawled on the floor wearing the ice cream from head to toe.

'Who's the Uber-goober now?' Cody thought. The elephant didn't even look back, but just flicked his tail good-bye.

"Cody," said Dad, "I want you to promise me something."

"Yes, Sir?" Cody asked.

"Promise me that you won't ever let those elephants come back. It doesn't matter what the problem is, we can handle it, but only if we're honest."

Cody looked relieved. "Yes, Sir."

"And remember, Son, elephants have very long memories . . . ."

"Yes, Sir!" Cody laughed.

The family looked around them at the mess

in the living room, and then Dad said, "Hmmm. I think a little vacation might be in order while we get someone in to clean this up. I'd say it will take them at least a week just to get rid of that smell. Then we'll see about new curtains and a coffee table."

"And don't forget about the lampshade!" his mother laughed. "Or, we could just move into the new house, I suppose. . ."

"What new house?" His dad smiled and opened the window to air out the smell.

......The End

About the Author

Shannon Fay is a storyteller who lives in New Orleans, Louisiana, USA.

A distant cousin of Peter Pan, she is a rather old child who still loves to climb trees, build sancastles, make snow angels and do tumblesets on the clouds with her grandboys, Zane & Brock.

Shannon has been a writer since she was 7 years old, and wishes that all children everywhere could believe that they are writers, too, with wonderful, magical stories of their own to tell (even if they aren't very good spellers).

www.ShannonFay.com

About the illustrator

Danny Deeptown is a professional UK based freelance illustrator who creates art for children and adults alike.

He is a avid believer in 'good ol drawing' inspired by master line artists such as E H Shepard, Ronald Searle and Quentin Blake.

He is a nature lover and wishes he had a similar upbringing to Mowgli from The Jungle Book....which he likes to believe is a true story.

When he's not busy creating in his studio, he likes to explore the English countryside whilst listening to 60's rock n roll music.

He has a best friend called Captain Bernatard...who's a cat!

www.DannyDeeptown.co.uk

Made in the USA
Middletown, DE
18 May 2022

65937923R00046